Oscar Armstrong Hills

The Golden Wedding of Mr. and Mrs. Darwin T. Hills

at Crawfordsville, Indiana, Nov. 18, 1878

Oscar Armstrong Hills

The Golden Wedding of Mr. and Mrs. Darwin T. Hills
at Crawfordsville, Indiana, Nov. 18, 1878

ISBN/EAN: 9783337734886

Printed in Europe, USA, Canada, Australia, Japan

Cover: Foto ©Andreas Hilbeck / pixelio.de

More available books at **www.hansebooks.com**

Golden Wedding

OF

Mr. and Mrs. Darwin T. Hills,

AT

CRAWFORDSVILLE, INDIANA,

NOV. 18, 1878.

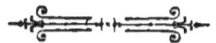

PREFATORY NOTE.

The following discourse was preached in the First Presbyterian Church of Crawfordsville, Ind., on Sabbath morning, November 17th, 1878. Invited by the esteemed pastor of the church, Rev. George C. Lamb, to occupy the pulpit that day, it was the author's filial desire shared by all the children, in this public way to signalize the goodness of God in bringing us to the "Golden Wedding" of our beloved and honored parents. The sermon was not intended for publication; but is printed in response to the wish of different members of the family to possess some permanent memorial of the auspicious day.

Advantage is taken of the printing to preserve also a historical sketch and register of the family, and some account of the anniversary festivities.

O. A. H.

ALLEGHENY, PA., *Nov.* 22d, 1878.

CONTENTS.

		PAGE.
I.	THE MEMORIAL SERMON, -	5
II.	THE HISTORICAL SKETCH, -	13
III.	THE GOLDEN WEDDING, -	17
IV.	THE FAMILY REGISTER, -	24

THE DIVINE DIRECTION AND DISCIPLINE.

By Rev. O. A. Hills, D. D.,

Pastor of the North Presbyterian Church, Allegheny, Pa.

" And thou shalt remember all the way which the Lord thy God led thee these forty years in the wilderness, to humble thee, and to prove thee, to know what was in thine heart, whether thou wouldest keep His commandments or no:"—Deuteronomy, viii: 2.

I am called to address you this morning, my friends, on an occasion of more than ordinary interest to many who now hear me. A "Golden Wedding"—of special concern to a single family in this congregation—will not be an unmarked event even to the entire church, where for more than twenty-five years one of the venerable parties has served in the eldership. With no offensive family pride, or undue obtruding upon the public of private affairs, I invite you to join the circle of children and kindred in setting up for our beloved and honored parents the " Ebenezer "—'*stone of help*,' while they say, with the patriarchal prophet, " Hitherto the Lord hath helped us."—1 Sam. vii : 12.

We stand, this morning, upon the dividing line between the past and future years. Our eyes are now turned backward. And to our grateful hearts one prominent theme is specially emphasized. We recall to-day, not our merits, worthiness, or high endeavors, but

The Divine Direction and Discipline.

These words of Moses to Israel embody important and suggestive features of this theme; and the journey of Israel through the desert furnishes their most pertinent and beautiful illustration. We, who believe, my brethren, are journeying to the land of light and love. Some of us are just beginning—their tottering steps and lisping lips indicating that it is still with them the day of childhood. Some of us are are in the midst of thorny ways and wicked enemies; and, with girded loins, and in the panoply of God, are seeking to do valiant service in his name and cause. Some of us are sitting in the shadows of the great mountains ; and the roll of Jordan's flood is even now filling the ear—ever sweet and grateful music, refreshing prelude of the heavenly anthem. Let us all this morning stop here a little while, surrounded with the thronging memories of half a century ; and looking back, note the characteristics and consequences of this Divine direction and discipline.

I. THE CHARACTERISTICS.

Moses charges the children of Israel to " remember all the way which the Lord their God led them forty years in the wilderness." And, resting on the slopes of Abarim, with the weary way now all behind them and Canaan just across the Jordan, they could not for a moment doubt the fact that an Almighty and gracious hand had brought them so near their journey's end.

1. *But with us, as truly as with them, the Divine guidance has been real.* They had, indeed, the pillar of cloud and of fire. It was a fitting symbol of the glorious, and dreadful, and gracious God. It indicated to them the general direction of their journey over the trackless sands. It went before them in every time of difficulty or doubt, and in the hour of danger stood between them and peril. It overshadowed them in the heat of the noon-day ; and it lighted them in the darkness of the night. It chose for them, with an infinitely tender care for the feeblest of them, their daily marching and their nightly rest.

We have had, my friends, no pillar-cloud to go before our way ; but the Divine direction has been as real to us as was ever that of Israel. Our pathway, thus far through all the years of life, has been made perfectly plain. The gracious hand of a loving Father has hitherto shaped and fashioned all our goings. The light of the sun was the smile of our God. When prosperity's sun was overclouded, we saw it was a gracious, grateful shade ; and in the darkest night God's guidance has been a pillar of light.

Our guidance, too, has been as minute as ever Israel's was. " The *steps* of a good man are ordered by the Lord."—(Psalm xxxvii : 23). And from our own experience, perhaps, we each can testify how often the turning of a hand, or the lifting of a foot, has changed the direction and even destiny of our lives.

To borrow an illustration from the family whose anniversary we commemorate ; I cannot say that our household came over the ocean in the Mayflower, but I am quite sure it came across the flood with

Noah! However this may be, a little less than three-quarters of a century ago, from the village of Farmington, in Connecticut, (which I recently had the pleasure of visiting,) a young physician, with a young wife and little boy two years of age, moved into the then unbroken wilderness of Central Ohio. The hand of God led them by a way they knew not. About the same time, from a retired spot in the Pan Handle of Virginia, another household, in which was found a little girl four years of age, saw the pillar of cloud and fire lifting and moving westward. That cloud rested not until it covered the place where the guidance of God soon after brought the other family. They knew it not; but the plan was of God to unite those families in the union of son and daughter—so establishing another household, which in fifty years should gather around the Stone of Help to magnify the goodness and loving kindness of the Lord.

Less than a hundred and fifty years ago, a little boy eleven years of age heard Whitefield preach in Newburyport, Massachusetts; and was converted through the instrumentality of the sermon. Suppose it had been said to Whitefield, "You were not very successful to-night; only one, and he a little boy, has been moved." The great evangelist might have retired to rest greatly disheartened, almost wondering if his work were not entirely done. Yet that boy grew to man's estate. God gave him a numerous family, which he trained for his glory; and of that family in successive generations there have come already sixteen ministers of the Gospel! Can we fail to believe that God's hand led that little boy's feet to the sanctuary that eventful night a little more than a hundred years ago?

Again, if I may, without offence, refer to our own family, I well remember a winter night, more than a quarter of a century since, in a little country woolen mill in South-western Ohio. A boy sat at the bobbin-wheel winding bobbins for the loom, where his father sat plying with ever steady stroke the flying shuttle. A messenger tossed a letter into the weaver's lap. The candles were burning to their sockets; the bobbin-wheel spun round and round; and the shuttle flew still back and forth. They knew it not; but that humble letter was but the edge of the pillar-cloud, swaying to and fro and lifting for its westward flight. It brought another family to this beautiful little city, and gave the bobbin-boy an opportunity to graduate at Wabash College; and to-day it is his joy to emphasize the guidance of a wise and loving hand he did not see. The incident illustrates the Divine direction, and no less the inestimable value of the College to the people of this city.

2. *With us, as with Israel, the Divine direction and discipline have often been unexpected.* There were two ways from Egypt to Canaan. The one ran by the sea-shore; and less than a week would have sufficed to accomplish the journey. The other was the way of the wilderness. It was a devious and difficult road. Moses himself describes it as " that great and terrible wilderness, wherein were fiery serpents, and scorpions, and drought; where there was no water." And God chose for Israel this longer way. In weariness they trod its every turn. " He found him in a desert land, and in the waste howling wilderness; he led him about, he instructed him, he kept him as the apple of his eye. As an eagle stirreth up her nest, fluttereth over her young, spreadeth abroad her wings, taketh them, beareth them on her wings; so the Lord alone did lead him, and there was no strange god with him."—(Deut. xxxii : 10-12).

Why did God thus lead and try his ancient people? In strange and unexpected ways he brought them on their journey. He did it to fit them for their inheritance. They wanted Canaan ; he wished to make them ready for it. They loved ease : he would inure them to a life of self-denial. After two centuries of bondage, with all the restraints of servitude removed, liberty to them meant license ; and they needed the discipline of forty years, as truly as our freedmen need to be taught the responsibilities that ever wait on privileges and opportunities. The way was mysterious ; but God was preparing them for their rest.

Is not this a picture of our lives, dear friends? The way by which the Lord has led you all these years, that now stretch back in long perspective, has been more difficult and far more tortuous than you ever expected it would prove, as you looked forward to it. You have often sung, in sadness,

> " My soul, with various tempests tossed,
> Her hopes o'erturned, her projects crossed,
> Sees every day new straits attend,
> And wonders where the scene will end."

As with Israel, you have been " continually surprised, perplexed, and even angered by the doings of God. It has seemed to you, at times, as if he had made the greatest possible mistakes, and as if the acts of his providence were in the most absolute contradiction to his word of promise."

But now, as you look back, can you not see the origin of all your trouble in your love of present comfort, and in your desire for immediate possession of the promised land? God means—has meant all the time—to give you this in some form or other: but he means besides to give you something more and better than even the longed-for Canaan. He designs a double mercy. Absent to prepare for you a place, he is present also to prepare you for the place. Therefore he leads you about, in a real but unexpected guidance, through the long and weary way of the wilderness.

3. *With us also, as with Israel, the Divine direction and discipline have often seemed very severe.* The journey of the wilderness was a continual "thorn in the flesh" to the ancient covenant people. There were the toilsome marches over the burning sands—the ever-recurring thirst—the daily gathering of manna, which, however pleasant in its novelty, became at last distasteful, and their "soul loathed the light food." There was the burdensome ritual, with its costly sacrifices, and ever smoking incense; and the severe chastisements for their sins. And oftentimes there came to them those weary waitings in the camp—more trying, as the soldiers tell us, than the painful march or the deadly shock of arms—when it seemed to them as if the pillar-cloud would never lift and point them to another stage of their pilgrimage.

Such, too, has been our life. The Divine discipline has often seemed severe. The severity has appeared, it may be, not so much in great afflictions as in a multitude of minor trials. In the heavy strokes we gird ourselves with the Divine strength which we seek; while in the daily round of trifling cares we do not ask nor do we get the heavenly help. But the lightest chain in time becomes intolerable; a continual dropping wears away the hardest rock. And God's disciplining stroke is oftentimes severest when apparently it is the lightest. This severity is specially felt in the anxieties of business—in the irritating pressure of hum-drum cares, that furnish little scope for the buoyancy of life—and, it may be, more than all, in those patience-trying calms of life, when our Heavenly Father lays his hand upon us, and in words, to be as little disobeyed as misinterpreted, says to us, "Now, my child, sir still." And to any parent who has tried to train a stirring four-year-old boy, it will be evident that this command is among the most difficult of implicit obedience. "They also serve who only wait:" but their's is not a service to be coveted.

These are the characteristics of the "Divine Direction and Discipline," most noticeable in the journey of Israel; and equally observable in the retrospect of our life, in the now well-nigh finished years. God has led us about in a guidance that has been real—in a way that we knew not—and in a discipline that has been wounding to the flesh and to the fleshly mind.

II. THE CONSEQUENCES.

What did God purpose to accomplish in this guidance and discipline of Israel? What was in his thought in leading and training us, as he has in the past? The text answers both questions at once.

1. *It was to teach us a knowledge of ourselves.* "To know what was in thine heart," are the words of Moses. It was a self-confident and irreligious host that went up out of Egypt. Recently neglected slaves, but now under the manifest guidance of Jehovah, what wonder if their hearts bounded from the lowest depths of despondency to the loftiest heights of a vain-glorious boasting.

Were we, my friends, less proud and unspiritual when God took us in hand to train us for his heavenly kingdom? Well does a discriminating writer say—" We know but little either of ourselves or of God. Our weaknesses, faults, and dangers, are, in a great degree, hidden from our view. 'Who can understand his errors?' Ignorant of what we are, we are equally so in reference to what we need, and most of all, ignorant of the best and most effectual processes and means by which our characters may be improved and our dangers escaped. Not only are our understandings limited, as those of creatures must needs be, but our minds are blinded by self-love, prejudice and pride; and nothing is more certain than that, if we were left to prescribe for own ease, and choose our own way, we should commit the most egregious and fatal blunders."

God's providential dealing with us thus opens up two worlds—the macrocosm of his mighty ways, where the great wheels of his providence are making their way to the desired Canaan—and the microcosm of our own souls, where we see what manner of spirit we are of. So God makes trial of us and proves us, and reveals us to ourselves; oftentimes unveiling that of which we did not even suspect the existence. When the faithful prophet revealed to Hazael the evil things which he was too soon to accomplish, the man amazed drew back and cried, "What! is thy servant a dog that he should do this thing?" The years rolled on to verify Elisha's words. Hazael was that very dog, to do those very things! The altered circumstances of God's providential appointment disclose what is in us; and so we come to know ourselves through the Divine leading.

2. *It was to make us humble and obedient.* Proud self-reliance is the besetting sin of all of us. It was a prime element in the first sin. It was a characteristic of ancient Israel. Nor is it less true of us. We are by nature proud, self-righteous, and self-satisfied and there-

fore do we need the discipline of numerous trials. Only so shall we
become obedient children, cheerfully keeping God's commandments.
The Christian is like the sandal-wood. Taking up the American Cy-
clopedia, the other day, to examine another reference, my eye fell upon
a picture of the sandal wood tree, and was arrested by a single suggestive sentence. You know this wood is exceedingly aromatic, used in
the manufacture of ladies' fans,—and among the heaviest and most durable of woods—so durable that the gates of an oriental temple made
of it still do good service though in use for more than a thousand years.
This is the sentence which arrested my attention: " The wood is very
heavy, its density and aroma being greatest when it grows on dry and
poor soil." And I thought God makes Christians as he makes the
sandal-wood. The knitting together of a firm and durable fibre, and
the storing away of the aroma that shall exhale its richest fragrance
for a thousand generations, require a poor earthly soil, which shall only
give it a place to grow, and make it the more evident that its sweetest
perfume comes not from the ground but from the skies!

3. *It was to teach us our dependence on God.* This was Israel's discipline. " He humbled thee, and suffered thee to hunger, and fed thee
with manna, which thou knewest not, neither did thy fathers know, that
he might make thee know that man doth not live by bread only, but
by every word that proceedeth out of the mouth of the Lord doth man
live." The life of Israel upon the banks of the Nile was very different from their experiences in the desert. The river made the land. Its
annual overflow brought them plenty. They were not dependent on
the fickle clouds or changing winds. The rising of the Nile measured
the bounty of their harvests. What wonder then that Egypt came to
worship the Nile: and not Him who on yon distant mountains stored
the floods that made the mighty river! And among such a people for
two hundred years Israel had been reared. Now they are taken to the
desert, and for forty years must look directly to an Almighty hand for
the supply of all their wants. The manna is given to them only day
by day; and their thirst is to be assuaged by water from the smitten
rock. Most effectually were they taught their absolute dependence
upon a higher power than their own. And they learned more than
their dependence for daily bread; they learned their need also of the
Divine Word. God's providences were a training to faith; and through
the lower they came to the higher, and learned that they must turn to
God for the satisfaction of all their spiritual cravings.

Does not God mean, my friends, by his disciplining guidance, that we shall learn the same lesson? We build up bulwarks about us; but they are only sand, and speedily crumble away. Among the old Saxons a favorite name for children was Ed-ward or Ed-win—signifying one who keeps or gains property. We retain the names and cherish the spirit of our fathers. We seek for them the wealth of men, by retaining what we give, or winning all they can. And so we gird them about with safeguards against the evil day. But it is too often all in vain. Our mighty bulwarks are like battlements of snow. They glisten in their glory it is true; but they are bound to melt in prosperity's sun, and flood or freeze the loved ones we desire them to defend. And our loved ones, even as ourselves, must learn, at last, through all vicissitudes and trials, that God Jehovah is alone our refuge and our strength.

CONCLUSION.

One other reason, brethren, is given in a subsequent verse, for this Divine leading and training of Israel, viz.:—"To do thee good at thy latter end."—viii: 16. And it was so. They saw it not; but, through all their painful wanderings, a gracious hand was shaping their way to "the land that flowed with milk and honey." Need I say we follow in their footsteps? From this high point we trace a strange and weary way; but a gracious, loving purpose has guided the march, ever ordaining the daily duty and the nightly rest. That purpose has been to "do us good at our latter end." The best and last of all this guidance and government is that God means to give us Canaan. The glorious end will soon and surely come. And when the wasting years are ended, we then shall see how for our good we have ever had

The Divine Direction and Discipline.

THE HISTORICAL SKETCH.

DARWIN TODD HILLS was born in the village of Farmington, Hartford County, Connecticut, December 6th, 1806—the year in which Dr. Noah Porter began his long ministry of sixty years in the pastorate of the Congregational Church of that place. His father was Dr. James Harvey Hills;* and his mother's name was Beulah Andrews.† His middle name is borne in honor of his father's sister's husband, Dr. Todd, the distinguished friend and educator of the blind. He was the third child and second son in a family of eleven ‡ children. When he was but two years of age, his father removed to Worthington, Franklin County, O., in 1808. Dr. Hills practiced medicine in Worthington for ten years, then for two years in Madison county, on the Big Darby, then for two years in West Liberty, Logan county, O. In April, 1822, he removed to Delaware, O., at the solicitation of many old friends; and continued in the practice of his profession until his death in 1830, at the age of 49. His widow, Darwin's mother, survived her husband thirty-six years, and died in Delaware, June 20th, 1866. At an early age Darwin was apprenticed to the business of woolen manufacturing, in which he has spent his life.

---

*Of our ancestors on the Hills' side, the writer of this has been unable, chiefly for want of time, to learn much beyond the fact that Dr. Hills' father is known to have had three brothers, at least. He (Dr. H.) was himself one of ten children, of whom eight (four boys and four girls) lived to grow up, marry, and leave children, "who are scattered all over the country from Vermont to New Orleans"—so says Mrs. Todd in the letter hereinafter quoted. She was the youngest of the eight.

†Beulah Andrews was the second of eight children, and the oldest daughter, of Moses Andrews, who "entered the army in the early part of the Revolution as paymaster of the 2d Reg't of the Connecticut Line. He was afterwards superintendent of Naval Affairs bordering Long Island Sound." He was one of nine children, of whom seven lived to maturity. His parents were Moses Andrews and Lydia Root of New Britain, Ct.

‡Their names were: 1. Ralph; 2. Joan; 3. Darwin; 4. Ralph; 5. Ralph; 6. Reuben; 7. Harvey; 8. Chauncey; 9. Rachel; 10. Mary; 11. Elnora. Of these, the first two Ralphs died in infancy. Joan married a Mr. Murray. She survived her husband many years, and spent her life in teaching. Among her pupils was his Excellency R. B. Hayes, President of the United States, who a few years ago, being then Governor of Ohio, joined the large circle of her friends and kindred in Delaware, O., as a mourner at her grave. Ralph (4) is a physician of distinction. For more than twenty years Superintendent of Lunatic Asylums at Columbus, O., and Weston, W. Va., he is now superintendent of the Ohio Reform School for Girls. Reuben, for many years a successful merchant at Oxford, O., died, just at the close of the recent war, in New Orleans, whither he had gone in the vain search for health. Harvey died young. Chauncey is a prominent citizen of Delaware, O., and the honored head of a family, which bids fair to rival in numbers that of his oldest brother. Rachel married a Mr. Perry Bunker, of Marion, O., and has been dead many years. Mary married Rev. David S. Anderson—the 2d in the list in the note on page 11. Elnora is the wife of Mr. Jasper Avery, a worthy citizen of Delaware, O.

Sarah Anderson was born in the village or settlement of Short Creek, Ohio county, in what is now West Virginia, in that portion commonly known as the Pan Handle—about midway between Wellsburg and Wheeling. Her father's name was Matthew Anderson, and her mother's Isabella Hughes.* She was the third daughter and seventh child in a family of thirteen† children. Sarah was born January 1st, 1805. Her father was an elder in the Presbyterian Church of Short Creek, which, at that time (the date of her birth) was united in one pastoral charge with the Presbyterian Church of Upper Buffalo, the pastor of the two churches being Rev. James Hughes, a brother of Sarah's mother. He afterwards became Dr. James Hughes, and died the first President of Miami University, Oxford, O. When Sarah was two years old, her father removed to St. Clairsville, O., where he resided six years, removing thence to Delaware, O., about the year 1812, and some ten years before Dr. Hills removed with his family to the same place.

The first acquaintance of our father and mother began in this place, —then an insignificant village in the midst of an almost unbroken wilderness. But long years were destined to elapse before their union.

The Providence of God led them about and watched over them in all their ways, and finally united them in marriage. This union took place in Oxford, Butler county, O.; the marriage being solemnized at 6 o'clock P. M., November 18th, 1828, at the house of Mr. Charles Barrows, whose wife was the bride's oldest sister; and who, long a resident of Oxford, now in Crawfordsville, Ind., at the age of eighty-one, finds a home with the sister whose married life began a half century ago under her own roof. The officiating minister was Rev. R. H. Bishop, D. D., then and for many years President of Miami University.

Thus united at the ages of twenty-two and twenty-three, the newly wedded pair made their first home on Cæsar's Creek, Green county, O., where, however, they remained but five months. In the spring of 1829

---

* Isabella Hughes' father's name was Rowland Hughes. He emigrated from England—though it is believed that the family came originally from Wales. The Hughes family is one of the Levitical families of the Presbyterian Church. Rowland had at least three sons in the ministry—James, Smiley, and Thomas Edgar. Two sons of James became ministers. Joseph S. and Thomas Edgar. Smiley died early. Four sons of Thomas Edgar (James' brother) became ministers—William, John D. Watson, and James Rowland. Two sons of Isabella became ministers—James H. Anderson and David S. Anderson. Then of the third generation, William has had three sons in the ministry—Thomas Edgar, Isaac M. and Melancthon; and a son of John D. died while studying Theology.

† Their names were: 1. William; 2. Alexander; 3. Mary; 4. Joseph; 5. Hughes; 6. Elizabeth; 7. Sarah; 8. Samuel; 9. Martha; 10. Tirzah; 11. James H.; 12. Thomas H.; 13. David S. James and David became Presbyterian ministers, as stated in the preceding note. Only four of the above list—Mary, Sarah, Thomas, and David—are now living.

they removed to Woodburn, Montgomery county, O., where they remained one year. Here their first-born son—Edwin Harvey, was given them, August 8th, 1829. In the spring of 1830 they removed to Bear Creek, eight miles south-west of Dayton, O. They lived at this point three years, during which their second son—Darwin Todd, Jr.—was born, on the twenty-fifth anniversary of his father's birth—December 6th, 1831. In April, 1833, they removed to Miamisburg, Montgomery county. O., where they remained nearly one year. This was the birthplace of their third son—Henry James—December 19th, 1833. In May, 1834, they removed to the neighborhood of Brownsville, Union county, Ind., where they continued to reside eight years, until 1842. During their residence at this place, four more sons were born to them, viz.: Richard Murray, December 8th, 1835; Oscar Armstrong, December 13th, 1837 ; David Anderson, April 21st, 1840, and Charles Barrows, February 9th, 1842. In the month of May, 1842, they removed to Richmond, Ind., where they remained two brief but memorable years. Here was born their eighth son—January 11th, 1844—Matthew, who lived but five days, dying January 16th—the first break in the large family circle. This first stroke of affliction in their home life was soon followed by, if possible, a more grievous one in the death of Charles, March 7th, 1844, at the age of two years and one month. One month later, with sorrowing hearts they left their dead in the beautiful little Quaker city, and returned to Ohio. They settled in Green county, at the village of Spring Valley, seven mile miles south-west of Xenia. Here they remained two years ; and here their ninth and youngest son, Francis Eugene, was born April 1, 1845. During their residence at this place, our parents united by certificate from Richmond with the Presbyterian Church of Xenia, in which soon after father was ordained a Ruling Elder—an office he has held continuously ever since. In the month of April, 1846, they removed to Caesar's Creek. in the same county, five miles east of Xenia, where they had begun their married life seventeen years before. They continued to reside at this point for six years. Here also their only daughter—the tenth and last child—Beulah Isabella—so named after the two grandmothers—was born October 18th, 1848.

In the spring of the year 1852, they removed again to Indiana, settling this time in Crawfordsville, Montgomery county. Here they have resided ever since ; and here it is the desire of their children that the wanderings of their earthly pilgrimage may finally cease. During their residence here, of more than a quarter of a century they have

seen all their children married, save the daughter, who, a graduate of
the Glendale, Ohio, Female College in the year 1869, in the honorable
profession of teaching, still remains at home, the comfort and joy of
our venerable parents' declining years.

The time would fail to make any full record of the last twenty-six
years. The successive marriages of the children and their present res-
idences will be found noted in the register. It is enough here to say
that their children number ten, of whom eight are living. They have
had thirty-one grand children, of whom twenty-six are yet alive; and
their descendants, counting the living and the dead, and those joined
to the family by marriage, number, at the end of their fifty years, just
fifty souls! "Lo, children are an heritage of the Lord; and the fruit
of the womb is his reward. As arrows are in the hand of a mighty
man, so are the children of the youth. Happy is the man that hath
his quiver full of them; they shall not be ashamed, but they shall
speak with the enemies in the gate."—(Psalm cxxvii: 3-5).

THE GOLDEN WEDDING.

The fifty years have sped rapidly away; and the shortening days of autumn bring quickly on the long expected anniversary. The golden printed cards, duly sent forth, have done their mission; and in the gloaming of the November evening (the 18th, at 6 o'clock), which needed only "the spitting of a little snow to make it like the original afternoon," four or five score friends gather in the little white cottage, No. 99 East Main street, to build the grateful Ebenezer. Besides the numerous friends from the beautiful little city, there were present from Delaware, O., Mr. and Mrs. Chauncey Hills, the bridegroom's youngest brother and his wife, and his two only living sisters, Mrs. Mary E. Anderson and Mrs. Elmora Avery. Mrs. Mary Barrows, the bride's only living sister, making her home with her, also must not be forgotten.

The following children were present, viz.:—Edwin and wife, Todd, Harry, Murray and wife, Oscar, and Beulah; and the grandchildren present were Eddie L. and Oscar—Clarence, Ida, Ernest, Lulu, Homer, Everett, Elmer, Whiteford and George—Charlie, Stella, Mamie and Emma—Miriam and Eddie R., that is just one-half the whole number of their descendants!

The venerable couple received their friends standing in the parlor alcove decorated with evergreens and autumn leaves, while above all shone out the flowered figures 28–78. It would have been a great joy to have had present the distinguished minister who solemnized the wedding of fifty years ago, but he has long since gone to the marriage supper of the Lamb. In his absence it was a great gratification to have his son, Rev. John M. Bishop of Lebanon, Ind., take his father's place, and give his benediction to his father's friends. This he did in a felicitous manner and with words fitly chosen. The company having all gathered, Mr. Bishop, lifting his eyes to the decorated arch, said:—

"Twenty-eight! Seventy-eight! We are assembled, my friends, to congratulate our brother and sister on this, the fiftieth anniversary of their marriage. I suppose my sainted father, who solemnized the cere-

inal wedding, said something like this : ' Marriage is both a Divine
ordinance and a civil contract. Instituted by God for the happiness of
his creatures, his blessing is to be sought upon this union.' Then, I
have no doubt, he engaged in prayer for the Divine benediction. I
will, therefore, ask you, Brother and Sister Hills, to join your right
hands, while Dr. Tuttle leads us in prayer."

Rev. Dr. J. F. Tuttle, President of Wabash College, then offered a
fitting prayer for the blessing of God upon his aged servants.

After prayer, Mr. Bishop continued :—

"On that occasion fifty years ago, my father put to you certain questions, the repetition of which is not now neceesary; but I will now ask
you whether you regret the promises then made?"

To this question the interested parties responded with an emphatic
negative. Whereupon, with a pertinent incident, the officiating minister invoked the continued blessing of the covenant-keeping God upon
the favored pair. Following which came the congratulations of the
numerous company.

During this part of the exercises, two large and elegant arm-chairs
were introduced into the alcove—a present from the grand-children—
on which the happy bride and groom were speedily seated. Soon after,
escorted to a bountiful supper, they passed by a table on which were
displayed other tokens of esteem, and were seated at the generous
board, only to lift their plates each from a pair of beautiful gold-
rimmed spectacles suited to the eyes of each—an appropriate and inex-
pensive present from their own children.

After supper, the usual postprandial exercises were called for, and
Mr. Bishop was introduced as the first speaker, with the statement that
he desired to ' finish his speech.' Referring to this, he said :—

"My friends, I am exceedingly sorry to bring any charge against
my brother for the statement just made : but I certainly said *Amen* in
the other room. I am not like those ministers of the olden time—as
my father, for example, though not as good a man by any means—who
finished their sermons with a ' *Finally;*' then, after some further remarks, came to the ' *Conclusion;*' and then, with additional reflections,
wound up with '*Now, one word more.*' I finished all I had to say before supper ; and in fact, I may as well confess it, I am now too full
for utterance! I will therefore only express my great gratification at
being permitted to join the festivities of this auspicious occasion, and
now gladly yield the floor to my Brother Hills "—with a wave of the
hand—" or, as we must distinguish them in some way, Dr. Hills."

Who suggested that ' Brother Hills ' would be sufficient to indicate the bridegroom. The said bridegroom, being then called for, made his way through the throng to his aged partner, saying *sotto voce*, ' I feel safer beside the old lady,' and spoke substantially as follows :—

" Friends and fellow citizens : Next to our gratitude to our Heavenly Father, I wish to thank you all for your kind presence—your golden faces, as well as your golden presents. The circumstances of this anniversary are very different from those of the wedding fifty years ago. The goodness of God to the Hills family has been very great, though very few of them have ever succeeded in obtaining a large amount of this world's goods. I remember receiving, in 1862, a letter from my aunt, Mrs. Catharine Todd,* of Hartford, Connecticut, in which she speaks of one of our ancestors selling a handsome farm in Connecticut for a considerable sum, and taking his pay in Continental money, which soon became worthless, except as uncouth playthings for the children. [Voices—' That must have been *fiat money*—' He is making a hard money speech ']. That was as near as any of us ever came to being rich! As to the original wedding, the day was very much such a day as this has been, except that then it was colder and was snowing. I had a long journey on horseback to reach Oxford. Col. Walter Perry (who still lives at Monmouth, Ill., and whom I should have been glad to welcome here to-night), accompanied me. We rode through Hamilton, the county seat, in order to get the license. And speaking of that reminds me that I have some doubts whether we were ever properly married ; and I-have had some fears, since coming to Indiana that the old lady might desert me. The clerk of the court was that day in Oxford, and no one in the office was authorized to attend to his business. After considerable trouble and parleying about the matter, a young man finally filled up the blank, affixed the seal, and signed the clerk's name ; and with the document thus prepared, we mounted our horses and journeyed on to our destination. This we reached in due time, and the marriage was consummated. But I am like my Brother Bishop, too full for utterance, and must give place to others."

Dr. Hills was then called for and said :—

" I give you fair warning, my friends, that if you expect to hear from all the Hills to-night you will have to stay a good while ; for there is no end to them. In fact, I sat down this morning to work out a very suggestive mathematical problem. The details of it I cannot give you,

* Who in the same letter speaks thus of our father: "You, whom I remember as a little lively blue-eyed boy of two or three years." She says also: "I could now show you the house, and I presume the very room, in which you were born.

but only the elements and result. It is a problem in geometrical progression. The first term is 2, the ratio is 5: and the unit of the number of terms is 25. The question is, How long can this thing be allowed to run? [Laughter.] I am glad to see you enjoying yourselves, but I wish to assure you, my friends, that, to those of you who do not belong to the Hills family, it is not a laughing subject at all! And I will demonstrate the matter thoroughly. Fifty years ago this couple started out, they two alone. In twenty-five years they had increased to ten : and this you observe is an increase of five-fold. In

u) fifty years they number fifty : which you see again is a five-fold increase in twenty-five years. Now, suppose this ratio is kept up hereafter, what is to be the future of this family? Let us see. You know it is about three hundred and seventy-five years since Columbus discovered America, and that event is still counted in modern history. It will not seem very long, then, before that period is repeated. How many of this family, now, do you suppose there will be at the end of, say three hundred and fifty years? Well, you must remember that the best statisticians estimate the present population of the world as being 1,300,000,000. But if we grow at the rate of a five-fold increase every twenty-five years, at the end of 350 years, it is perfectly certain that there will be more than 2,400,000,000 of the Hills family alone! And if they are to find room for their increasing multitudes in that near future they must soon begin killing off the rest of mankind! I submit, therefore, the matter to your sober judgment as a thing by no means to be laughed at! But seriously it is a notable fact that upon this fiftieth anniversary we number just fifty* souls. Of these, eight are on the other shore, and the large majority of the remainder are present to-night. I agree with my father that the goodness and mercy of God have followed us all our days. We now number eight families—two of four each in Kansas, one of six in Missouri, one of five in Pennsylvania, and the others of three, four, twelve and six respectively are located in this city. In the last generation we counted Delaware, O., the center of the Hills family ; but in this generation that center has *gone west*—the great stream flowing at present from Crawfordsville and the old center supplying now only collateral rivulets." (To this last statement the truth of history compels the writer to say the Delaware delegation entered a most emphatic demurrer). The speaker recalled a number of reminiscences of the children's early life, which cannot here be re-produced, and concluded by saying, " But I must not monopolize the even-

---

* This statement is to be understood as not including the original pair.

ing. I wish to express my own great gratification with this joyous occasion, and to tender the thanks of all the children to the friends who have honored it with their presence. And with much joy to our beloved parents, I yield the floor to Dr. Tuttle."

Who in a few chosen and friendly words congratulated the happy host and hostess on the completion of a half century of wedded life.

Prof. John L. Campbell, of Wabash College, was next called upon, and responded in a brief and pertinent incident. Rev. Mr. Lamb and others were also summoned to the floor, but succeeded in evading the call.

At the suggestion of Mr. Bishop the company then joined in singing the Long Metre Doxology, after which he pronounced the benediction, and soon after the greater part of the company dispersed.

The remainder, consisting chiefly of the kindred, gathered in the parlor, unwilling as yet to close the happy day. It was suggested that the grandchildren had not yet been heard from. Immediately there were prolonged calls for Clarence (a graduate of Wabash College in 1876, and at present studying theology in Cincinnati), who rose and responded as follows:—

"My friends: The remarks, which I am called upon to make at this time, shall be entirely upon the spur of the moment, and upon no other point. Standing at the head of the third generation, I hope I have not presumed too much in taking to myself the title of Brigadier General of the army of grandchildren! This office, however worthily deserved, is not cheerfully conceded by all. Some are physically qualified for it, but have not the years and experience. To such I may say that it is not an easy position to hold. It might be said that the follies of the younger members of this generation are due in part to the *early* defects of the older members. And yet much may be said in commendation of this generation. In numbers we certainly present a respectable front. All told, we number thirty-one—twenty-six living and five dead. In educational matters we also present a respectable appearance. Two of us hold the degree of A. B. (whatever that may be). Two others have attended college to some extent, and now occupy the position of pedagogues. Another has attended a Female Seminary, and also an Academy of Music. This one was the first of our number to get married (Mrs. W. E. Stanley, Wichita, Kansas). Others are engaged in various mercantile and mechanical pursuits, while the great majority of our younger members are now in the process of education. The question has been asked me, why this third generation is still of the grandchildren? A due attention to emphasis would answer the question. It must be because they are *grand*-children! We feel, at any rate, that we are worthy offsprings of our worthy sires. I have nothing further to add, and will give way to my cousin collegian, who now has the floor prepared to make a speech."

Whereupon, responding to the general call, Edwin (also a graduate of Wabash College, in 1878), rose from his recumbent position—rendered necessary by the scarcity of chairs at hand—and said :—

" I have not had even the small advantage of my cousin, for preparing to speak on this occasion : but I do not propose to be outdone by any one who appends an A. B. to his name. I agree with my cousin's general estimate of this third generation ; and I suppose we must concede his claim to be the oldest grandchild. But he cannot monoplize all the honors of our generation : for I must inform you that I myself claim to be *the oldest son of the oldest son!* It has been already said that we number among our respectable race some worthy pedagogues, and as I have nothing further to say, I will give way to them."

Repeated calls then brought the third speaker to the floor ; and Charles spoke in substance as follows :—

"I feel as if I ought to stand up for those of our number who have been called *pedagogues*. Why they alone should be so called I am unable to say, for there are other pedagogues here besides them. And certainly I think it better to be a pedagogue than a demagogue. It is true we have no A. B. following our names; but I wish to say we have attended College somewhat—have rubbed our heads against it a little. We are now trying to rub that knowledge into the heads of other people In conclusion, I feel bound to say that, while I am not the oldest grandchild, nor the oldest son of the oldest son, *I am the son of my father, and the best boy my mother has got.*" (The others are girls !)

The other teacher—Ernest—was also called on, and responded in a neat brief speech, which unfortunately has escaped the reporter's recollection. The best things oftentimes, like the fragrance of flowers, delight us, and yet slip from our grasp.

So closed the Golden Anniversary. The sombre and leaden sky of the November evening was full of the rifted and breaking clouds as the guests assembled. And as the last of them stepped from the little portico, the bands of Orion bejeweled the frame of one of the unveiled stars shone out prophetic of the sunny to-morrow. And that morrow came with the rising of a glorious sun, that ushered in another stage of life's long journey. So, pray the children and the children's children, may every cloud disappear from life's horizon to our dear father and mother, so "that at evening time it shall be light," (Zech. xiv: 7); while even then the stars of the night shine, most of all, as the sure heralds of the dawning of an everlasting morning.